For Jess and Kat,
my two best girls xx - CH

For Olive - TN

SIMON & SCHUSTER
First published in Great Britain in 2021 by Simon & Schuster UK Ltd
1st Floor, 222 Gray's Inn Road, London, WC1X 8HB
Text copyright © 2021 Caryl Hart • Illustrations copyright © 2021 Tony Neal
The right of Caryl Hart and Tony Neal to be identified as the author and
illustrator of this work has been asserted by them in accordance with the
Copyright, Designs and Patents Act, 1988 • All rights reserved, including the
right of reproduction in whole or in part in any form • A CIP catalogue record for
this book is available from the British Library upon request.
978-1-4711-8269-3 (PB) • 978-1-4711-8271-6 (eBook)
Printed in China • 10 9 8 7 6 5 4 3 2 1

MiNi MONSTERS

Can I be the best?

CARYL HART & TONY NEAL

SIMON & SCHUSTER

London New York Sydney Toronto New Delhi

"My go! My go!" said Sparkle.

She took a deep breath and threw the dice.

"Shall we play again?" asked Sparkle.

But Arthur was too busy . . .

Outside, Scout was in the sand pit.

"Let's have a sandcastle competition!" he said.

"**Oh yes!** I'm **really** good at sandcastles!" cried Sparkle.

But Arthur's castle just wouldn't stick together.
When the others had finished,
Arthur said,

"Those are the best sandcastles
I've ever seen!"

The three friends set
off across the grass . . .

under the
climbing frame . . .

and past the
big umbrella.

. . . Scout crossed the finish line first.

"I won! I won!" he cried.

Sparkle was close behind.

"Wow!" she puffed. "You really are **best** at running!"

"You were both so fast," said Arthur

and he sat down on the grass looking sad.

"What's the matter, Arthur?" Sparkle asked.

Arthur sighed.

"You are the best at games and sandcastles

 and Scout is the best at running . . .

but I'm not the **best** at anything."

"Well, you must be best at something?" said Sparkle.

But she didn't know what.

Arthur plodded over to the big tree to be by himself.

"Arthur is sad," said Sparkle.
"He thinks he's not good at anything."

"Oh dear," sighed Scout.
Then, he spotted something in the grass.

It gave him a wonderful idea!

Meanwhile, under the big tree,
Arthur found a little ladybird.
It was caught in a spider's
web and couldn't get free.

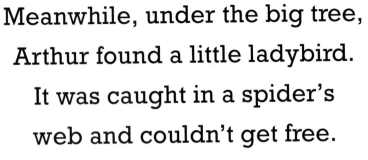

"Poor thing!"

He found a feather and
carefully broke the web.
"There you go,"
he smiled.

The ladybird waved its little feet to say thank you, then opened its wings and flew away.

Sparkle and Scout were racing around the garden gathering twigs and stones and pieces of wood.

"What are you doing?" asked Arthur.

"**We know what you're the best at!**"
Scout smiled.

"Really?" said Arthur.
"What?"

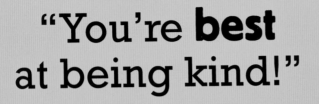

"You're **best** at being kind!" smiled Sparkle.

"Look how kind you are to insects!"

"And," said Scout, "you're always kind to us, even when you don't win!"

Arthur grinned happily.

And everyone agreed that being the best was nice, but being **BEST FRIENDS** was even better!